# A CANDLE IN THE WINDOW

This book is dedicated to Norene Memmott Ashman,
whose unwavering faith and unconditional love have blessed the lives of her family with miracles.
I love you, Grandma.

—Michele Ashman Bell—

To my family, to my husband, David, and to Margaret Weber
for all their love, patience, and support.

—Natalie Cannon Malan—

Cover design © 2006 by Covenant Communications, Inc.

Published by Covenant Communications, Inc.
American Fork, Utah

Printed in China
First Printing: October 2006

12 11 10 09 08 07 06    10 9 8 7 6 5 4 3 2 1

ISBN 1-59156-570-7

# A CANDLE IN THE WINDOW

Written by MICHELE ASHMAN BELL

Illustrated by NATALIE CANNON MALAN

Covenant Communications, Inc.

Nothing was the same for John after Molly died.

She passed away that spring of 1909, just as the earth was awakening from its winter slumber.

John worried for his three daughters, but it was eight-year-old Emily who concerned him the most, especially as the first Christmas without Molly approached. Emily knew her mother was gone but somehow hadn't seemed to grasp the concept of the finality of death. Emily was certain that Heavenly Father was going to let her mother come to visit her at Christmas.

"Mama visited me in my dream last night, Papa," Emily told him one morning. "She looked ever so beautiful. Her hair was long and shiny, and she laughed and played with me. Sometimes I'm sad that Mama left, but in the dream she was happy, so I wasn't sad anymore. She promised she would visit me on Christmas. Isn't that wonderful, Papa?"

John didn't know what to say. Emily's faith didn't waver—she was convinced it was true. He held her close and rocked her, wishing in his own heart that Molly would indeed come home.

The first Saturday in December, John and the girls, Sarah, Catherine, and Emily, bundled up and went into the hills above their town to select a Christmas tree, just as they'd done every year. After picking out a beautiful tree, they dragged it home, their breath creating spirals of steam in the cold air.

$L$ater that evening, while John went to the barn to do the chores, the girls began stringing together fluffy white popcorn and bright red cranberries.

Just as their mother had always done, Catherine lit a candle and put it in the window to help her father find his way back to the house through the darkness.

The decorations were strung about the fragrant limbs of the tree, and when their father returned from doing the chores, he helped the girls fasten candles to the branches—candles that would be lit on Christmas Eve.

"Mama would like this very much," John said as he gave each of his daughters a hug.

Christmas Eve morning after breakfast, John made an announcement. "I have a special surprise for you today."

"What is it, Papa?" Emily asked, wide-eyed.

"You'll see," he said as he placed a bundle on the settee and began unwrapping it. "Your mother made these for you," he said. "She wanted me to save them for you until Christmas."

Tears welling up in their eyes, the girls stared speechless at the matching dresses. Lifting the dresses one by one, John handed one to each daughter. The dresses were of rich, red wool plaid, with belts, cuffs, and collars made out of black velvet.

$W$ith tears and smiles, the girls hugged their papa, who couldn't stop tears from streaming down his own face. John cleared his throat. "Well, now, that's not quite all of it. Cover your eyes," he instructed.

Each daughter opened her eyes and saw a pair of patent-leather shoes, pretty enough for a princess. "Ohhh," Emily said breathlessly. "They are the most beautiful shoes I've ever seen. Can we wear them to the celebration tonight?"

"You can carry them with you to the church and wear your winter boots. Then you can change there."

Emily threw her arms around her father's neck and squeezed tightly. "Thank you, Papa," she said softly.

When they arrived at the church, they greeted their friends and neighbors, then hurried toward Grandma and Grandpa, who pulled the girls into big bear hugs.

"How lovely you look," Grandma said.

Emily and her sisters had almost forgotten that they had also brought their new shoes in their coat pockets, and they all rushed back to the coatroom to change their shoes. Grabbing a shoe out of her right pocket, Emily reached into the other pocket, but to her horror, her shoe was gone.

"My shoe," she cried. "It's gone." Sarah ran to find her father, and soon the whole family was searching for the missing shoe.

"Go have fun at the party. I'll find your shoe," John told her confidently.

A small, five-piece band on the stage struck up a happy tune, and couples took to the dance floor, sashaying and whirling about. Emily kept one eye on the door and one eye on the dance floor.

"Well, well," a deep voice said behind her. "I don't believe we've had a chance to dance yet this evening."

Emily turned to find her grandfather. "Hi, Grandpa," she said sadly.

"Your papa will find your shoe. How about we take a turn out on the dance floor, then fetch something to wet our whistles?"

Grandfather took Emily by the hand and guided her to the dance floor. He swung her around, making her feel light and airy. For a moment she forgot about her lost shoe.

*S*everal dances later, Emily caught a glimpse of her father standing in the doorway. She ran from the dance floor toward him. By the look on his face, she knew he hadn't found it.

He shook his head sadly, then said in an encouraging tone, "But I'm going back out to look. I just came inside to ask your grandfather to take you girls home for me."

When the party ended, the sisters bundled up and stepped outside into the thickly falling snow. Emily could feel her heart grow heavy, knowing that the new snow would cover any trace of her shoe.

"*P*apa must still be out looking," Catherine said when they arrived to an empty home.

"I'll stoke up the fire," Grandpa said. "You girls go change into your nightclothes. I'm sure your papa will be home soon."

After her sisters changed and left, Emily climbed off her bed, knelt down, and clasped her tiny hands together.

"Dear Heavenly Father, it's me, Emily. I don't mean to bother you, but I lost a shoe. It's a special shoe, from my mama. She lives with you now, but she said she would come and visit me tonight. Could you please ask her if she would help find my shoe?"

*J*ust as Emily joined her sisters and grandfather in the kitchen, the door opened and her father stepped inside. His face was pink from the cold, and he was covered with snow.

"I'm sorry, sweetie," he told his youngest. "I looked every inch of the way from our house to the church. It's just not there." His voice was sad and desperate.

"Don't be sad, Papa," Emily said, rising to give her father a hug. "It's okay."

Her father smiled at her and hugged her tightly. "That's my brave girl," he said.

After her sisters went to bed, Emily crept downstairs and found her father sitting in his rocker, staring at the fire with a lonely, faraway look in his eye. She almost turned and went back to bed, but he turned his head and saw her. Without a word, he held out his arms and Emily went to her father and sat on his lap, wrapped in his safe, strong arms.

"Papa?" Emily asked in a soft voice. "Would it be okay if I put a candle in the window?"

Her father looked at her, surprised. "Why do you want to do that?"

"So Mama can find her way home," she explained. "Is that all right?"

John nodded slowly and finally found his voice. "Yes, angel, it is."

Together they lit the candle and placed it in the windowsill, where its flickering light reflected brightly in the glass.

The next morning, Sarah and Catherine woke Emily from a deep sleep. She'd almost forgotten it was Christmas morning.

"Come on, Emily," Sarah coaxed as they descended the stairs. "What's in your stocking?"

Emily reached inside and pulled out a lovely rag doll with shoe-button eyes, long golden hair made of yarn, and a dress from the same material as her Christmas dress.

Emily couldn't speak. No one had to tell her that her mother had made this doll for her. She knew it, and she also knew she would treasure this doll forever. She would name her Molly.

After the gifts had all been opened, Sarah announced that she was going to make a special breakfast of hotcakes and sausages. Catherine's job was to set the table, and Emily's was to fetch wood off the back porch to build a fire in the cookstove. Holding Molly in one arm, Emily opened the back door, bracing herself for the cold morning air. Suddenly she cried out in joy.

"What is it?" Catherine asked as she rushed over to Emily's side. There, looking as good as new, was Emily's lost shoe.

"See," Emily announced, smiling as she picked up the shoe. "Mama did come. She brought me my shoe, just like I knew she would."

*I*n the years that followed, none of them ever forgot how special that Christmas was. Emily knew with all her heart that her mother had looked down from heaven that night and had seen the candle in the window.